Copyright © 1991 by Inga Moore
All rights reserved. No part of this book may be reproduced or
transmitted in any form or by any means, electronic or mechanical,
including photocopying, recording, or by any information storage and
retrieval system, without permission in writing from the Publisher.
Macmillan Publishing Company
866 Third Avenue, New York, NY 10022
First published by Andersen Press Ltd., London, England.
First American Edition 1991
Printed in Italy

10  9  8  7  6  5  4  3  2  1

Library of Congress CIP data is available.
ISBN 0-02-767648-X

# Little Dog Lost

*Written and illustrated by*
# Inga Moore

Macmillan Publishing Company • New York

Maxwell Macmillan International Publishing Group • New York • Oxford • Singapore • Sydney

When Dad got a new job in the country, I was so excited I could hardly wait to pack up all our pots and pans and move to our new house in the hills.

It was sad saying goodbye to everyone – especially my friend Jill. As we drove along, I wrote her a letter. It wasn't a long letter, because Pip kept looking out of the window and I had to hold onto him. Dad said I could have a real country dog now we were moving.

"But I *have* a real dog," I said. And Pip barked at him as if to say 'You bet'.

We drove right up into the hills.
"You would like it here, Jill," I wrote.
"Everything is really green and you can see for miles."

At last we reached our new house. It looked much nicer than our old one back on Bickley Street.

I told Jill I would write again soon and I signed my letter,

"Lots of love,
Liz xxx"

But it was a long time before I wrote to Jill again. I didn't like living in the country.

"It's so lonely," I told her. "I miss all my friends in town."

Tom and I knew everyone on Bickley Street. Now we were called city kids and no one would play with us. The only friend we had was Pip.

Jill loved Pip.

"He's just as funny as ever," I wrote. "He still sleeps in Grandpa's slipper and last week he rode home in my bicycle basket. But you'll never guess what. Mom bought an old piano for Grandpa to play and whenever we have a sing along, Pip joins in. He doesn't always sing in tune," I said, "but I wish you could hear him."

It was my birthday in the late autumn and Grandpa said perhaps Pip could sing at my party.

"Oh Grandpa," I said. "How *can* I have a party? I have no one to invite. I don't think I'll ever make new friends."

"You will," he said. "You'll see."

But autumn came and we still had no one to play with. Tom and I just stayed at home on our own. Grandpa said we should be more like Pip who loved living in the country and was always scampering off to explore.

Then, the night before my birthday, Pip disappeared. I couldn't find him anywhere.

Mom told me to try not to worry. But autumn was turning to winter and I kept imagining him wandering all alone in the cold and dark.

Then it began to snow.

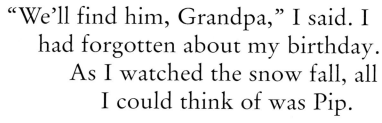

Poor Grandpa didn't play his piano at all that night. He just sat by the fire not saying a word.

"We'll find him, Grandpa," I said. I had forgotten about my birthday. As I watched the snow fall, all I could think of was Pip.

Next morning, as soon as it stopped snowing, Tom and I searched the woods behind our house.

"Look, tracks," said Tom. "Do you think they're Pip's?" I didn't know.

We followed them anyway, until we reached Hill Farm. That was where Lou and Cassie lived.

"They're the ones who call us names," said Tom.

"I don't care," I told him. "We have to find Pip." And I showed them his photo.

"What a funny little dog," laughed Cassie. "Look Lou." Lou said perhaps their brother, Ben, had seen him, but he hadn't and he said the tracks weren't Pip's. I was disappointed and turned to go.

"Wait," called Ben. "Can't *we* help you find your dog? Come on. Let's ask around. Someone must have seen him."

We went from house to house, asking the children who lived round about if they had seen Pip. None of them had but they *all* came to help us look for him.

As we walked along, I told them about the funny things Pip did. I don't think Cassie believed me when I said he could sing.

"I'd like to hear *that*!" she said.

We looked everywhere – in rabbit holes, fox holes,
in all the hollow logs. We searched the woods…

...and tramped the fields for hours.
But there wasn't a sign of him.

By now it was getting late, and the snow was starting
to fall again, when suddenly I heard a shout.
"Over here!" cried Ben. "I've found some
tracks!" They led all the way to the village.
"Are you sure they're Pip's?" I asked. It
seemed such a long way for a little dog to run.

But in the village the snow had covered
the trail. We asked at all the houses.
No one had seen Pip.

We were tired. We had all had enough,
and now the snow was falling heavily.

I couldn't go home without Pip,
but I didn't know where else to look.

"Perhaps we'll find him tomorrow,"
said Cassie. But I knew we wouldn't.

Then, as we stood quietly, I heard
a piano playing in the distance,
and voices singing…

I thought I heard a sound I knew.
I ran towards it and pushed open
a door…

And there was Pip singing at the top of his voice.
He was at the village choir practice!

I explained that Pip had disappeared and that we had been searching for him all day. Then, in came Tom with Cassie and the others. Tom told everyone it was my birthday and the next thing I knew I was having a party.

It was the best party I have ever had. Pip joined in singing Happy Birthday and everybody clapped and cheered.

Cassie looked *very* surprised. Then she smiled and said "Will you bring him over to play tomorrow?" I said we would.

I tucked Pip safely inside my coat and we set off home.

. . . .

"D'you know," I wrote to Jill late that night, "Grandpa was right. We *should* have been more like Pip. And now, thanks to Pip, I have so many new friends, I'm going to like living in the country after all."

I said I hoped she would come and stay with us soon and I signed my letter,

"Lots of love, Liz xxxx"